the blood of carthage

the blood of carthage

based on the television series created by
JOSS WHEDON

writer **CHRISTOPHER GOLDEN**

penciller **CLIFF RICHARDS**

inker **JOE PIMENTEL**

Sunnydale flashbacks by **CHYNNA CLUGSTON-MAJOR**

Carthage flashbacks by **PAUL LEE & BRIAN HORTON**

colorist **GUY MAJOR**

letterers **AMADOR CISNEROS & DRAGON MONKEY**

This story takes place during Buffy the Vampire Slayer's third season.

Titan books

publisher
MIKE RICHARDSON

editor
SCOTT ALLIE
with ADAM GALLARDO

collection designer
KEITH WOOD

art director
MARK COX

special thanks to
DEBBIE OLSHAN AT FOX LICENSING,
CAROLINE KALLAS AND GEORGE SNYDER AT *BUFFY THE VAMPIRE SLAYER*,
AND DAVID CAMPITI AT GLASS HOUSE GRAPHICS.

PUBLISHED BY
TITAN BOOKS
144 SOUTHWARK STREET
LONDON SE1 0UP

what did you think of this book? we love to hear from our readers.
please e-mail us at readerfeedback@titanemail.com or write to
Reader Feedback at the address above.

FIRST EDITION
MAY 2001
ISBN: 1 - 84023 - 281 - 1

1 3 5 7 9 10 8 6 4 2

printed in singapore.

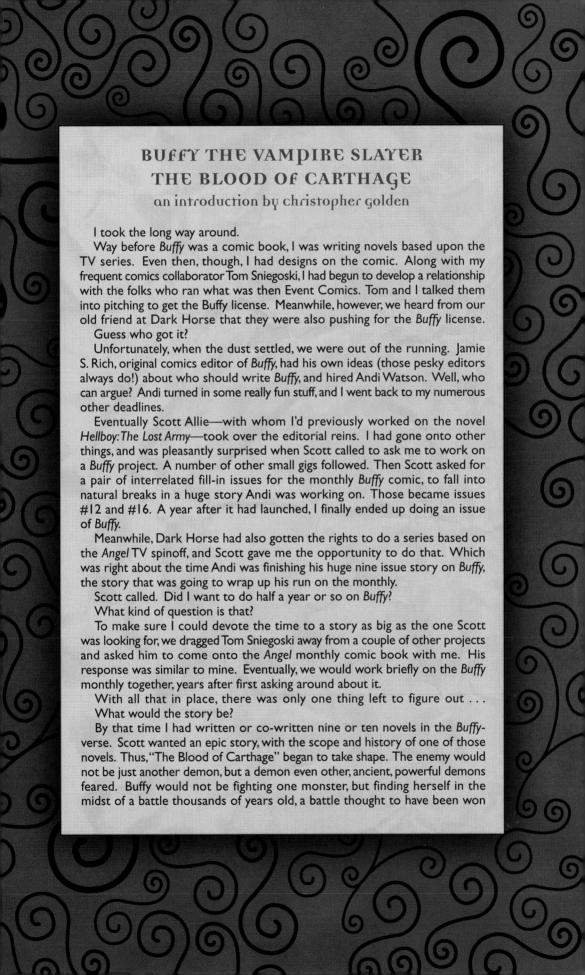

BUFFY THE VAMPIRE SLAYER
THE BLOOD OF CARTHAGE
an introduction by christopher golden

I took the long way around.

Way before *Buffy* was a comic book, I was writing novels based upon the TV series. Even then, though, I had designs on the comic. Along with my frequent comics collaborator Tom Sniegoski, I had begun to develop a relationship with the folks who ran what was then Event Comics. Tom and I talked them into pitching to get the Buffy license. Meanwhile, however, we heard from our old friend at Dark Horse that they were also pushing for the *Buffy* license.

Guess who got it?

Unfortunately, when the dust settled, we were out of the running. Jamie S. Rich, original comics editor of *Buffy*, had his own ideas (those pesky editors always do!) about who should write *Buffy*, and hired Andi Watson. Well, who can argue? Andi turned in some really fun stuff, and I went back to my numerous other deadlines.

Eventually Scott Allie—with whom I'd previously worked on the novel *Hellboy: The Lost Army*—took over the editorial reins. I had gone onto other things, and was pleasantly surprised when Scott called to ask me to work on a *Buffy* project. A number of other small gigs followed. Then Scott asked for a pair of interrelated fill-in issues for the monthly *Buffy* comic, to fall into natural breaks in a huge story Andi was working on. Those became issues #12 and #16. A year after it had launched, I finally ended up doing an issue of *Buffy*.

Meanwhile, Dark Horse had also gotten the rights to do a series based on the *Angel* TV spinoff, and Scott gave me the opportunity to do that. Which was right about the time Andi was finishing his huge nine issue story on *Buffy*, the story that was going to wrap up his run on the monthly.

Scott called. Did I want to do half a year or so on *Buffy*?

What kind of question is that?

To make sure I could devote the time to a story as big as the one Scott was looking for, we dragged Tom Sniegoski away from a couple of other projects and asked him to come onto the *Angel* monthly comic book with me. His response was similar to mine. Eventually, we would work briefly on the *Buffy* monthly together, years after first asking around about it.

With all that in place, there was only one thing left to figure out . . . What would the story be?

By that time I had written or co-written nine or ten novels in the *Buffy*-verse. Scott wanted an epic story, with the scope and history of one of those novels. Thus, "The Blood of Carthage" began to take shape. The enemy would not be just another demon, but a demon even other, ancient, powerful demons feared. Buffy would not be fighting one monster, but finding herself in the midst of a battle thousands of years old, a battle thought to have been won ages ago, but now taken up again in the present day, with the population of Sunnydale, and possibly the world, in the balance.

And . . . it's kinda her fault.

That was the other thing Scott and I talked about. "The Blood of Carthage" would move the comics continuity into the fourth season of the TV show. That meant Buffy was in college now, and having a difficult time balancing her destiny as the Slayer with the demands of higher education. With all that stress, she would be bound to make some mistakes, both in college and in Slayage, as she learned to find that balance.

One of those mistakes would turn out costly.

Fourth season also meant changes in the lineup of the "Scooby Gang." No Oz, for instance. But his absence is more than made up for by the presence of Spike, who plays a major role in "Blood of Carthage," something Scott and I agreed upon from the beginning. Anya would also play a role for the first time in the comics. Though minor, her presence was not only refreshing, but played into the overall plot of the story. Where are Riley and Tara, you may ask? Well, they're around. They're just not in here, 'cause at the time these issues were being plotted, we had no idea how long they would be alive, or even if they were really on Buffy's side or not.

One of the other things I try to do, whenever possible, is connect my own work in the *Buffy*-verse in such a way that you don't NEED to read the connected stories, but if you have, some of what follows might mean more to you. For instance, in "The Blood of Carthage" you'll see Brad Caufield, from #12 and #16, finally get to the end of HIS particular story arc. You'll meet the ghost of Lucy Hanover and the demon Tergazzi from the novel *Immortal*. And it works the other way around, too. Giles's actions in this story have repercussions in the *Giles* one-shot Tom Sniegoski and I wrote.

It's a big story. 114 pages, most of them beautifully illustrated by Cliff Richards. There are sweet flashbacks by Chynna Clugston-Major, and nasty ones by Brian Horton and Paul Lee, but just the idea that three different art styles went into the storyline is testament enough that Scott and I were trying for something big. I'd ask for a round of applause for all of those amazing artists, but I don't want you to put the book down just yet.

Anyway, like I said, it's a big story, with enough characters and history and globe-trotting and different story threads that I actually think we did what we set out to do—we created a novel in comic book form. That said, I also think it reads a lot better all put together like this than it did in chunks separated by thirty day intervals. But you'll have to be the judge of that.

Well, that's it. I took the long way around, no question, but I finally got my crack at this series. I hope you enjoy it, and I hope you'll come back for more.

Meanwhile, take a lesson from Buffy. We all make mistakes.

Just be happy yours don't usually bring about the apocalypse.

Christopher Golden
Bradford, Massachusetts
Halloween, 2000

SUNNYDALE. SUBURBIA WITH THAT SOUTHERN CALIFORNIA EDGE.

IT OUGHTA BE A POSTCARD.

BUT A PICTURE WILL NEVER SHOW THE TRUE FACE OF THIS TOWN, THE SHADOWS WITHIN. SUNNYDALE HAS A DARK HEART.

HERE, THE BARRIERS THAT SEPARATE THE HELLISH LANDS WHICH EXIST JUST AN EYEBLINK OUT OF SYNCH WITH OUR OWN WORLD ARE THINNER, THE DEMON DIMENSIONS CLOSER.

IN SIMPLEST TERMS, SUNNYDALE'S AN EVIL MAGNET.

A NICE PLACE TO VISIT. AS LONG AS YOU'RE GONE BY SUNDOWN.

THE SUN SETS IN THE WEST. THAT MEANS IF YOU'RE HEADED EAST, OUT OF TOWN, ON INTERSTATE 17, AND THE NIGHT IS SPREADING OUT BEHIND YOU...

YOU MIGHT JUST BE ABLE TO OUTRUN IT.

SUNNYDALE Twin Drive In

GAZ

OF COURSE, IT WON'T BE DARK FOR A WHILE YET.

FUN IN THE SUN, A JELLYSTONE-PARK-SIZE PICNIC, BONFIRE AFTER DARK... IT'S ALL GOOD.

ALL WORK AND NO PLAY MAKES BUFFY A DULL SLAYER. BUT I HOPE YOU DON'T THINK I'M JUMPING IN THERE.

PONDER OUR LACK OF APPROPRIATE SWIMMING ATTIRE, BUFF. I MAY BE MR. TOWNIE NOW, BUT JUST BECAUSE I DON'T GO TO COLLEGE, DOESN'T MEAN I'M STUPID.

THIS PLACE IS CREEPY ENOUGH WITHOUT THE X-TREME SPORTS, THANK YOU.

YOU'RE NOT KIDDING. WHAT IS THAT THING, ANYWAY?

HEY, BUFFY! HI!

FELICIA! HEY, HOW'VE YOU BEEN?

SOBER. BUT I'M BETTER NOW. WANT ONE?

MMM, NO, BUT THANKS. ME AND BEER HAD A KIND OF FALLING OUT. WE'RE NOT ON DRINKING TERMS ANYMORE.

YOU STILL WORKING AT THE POPSICLE PARLOR?

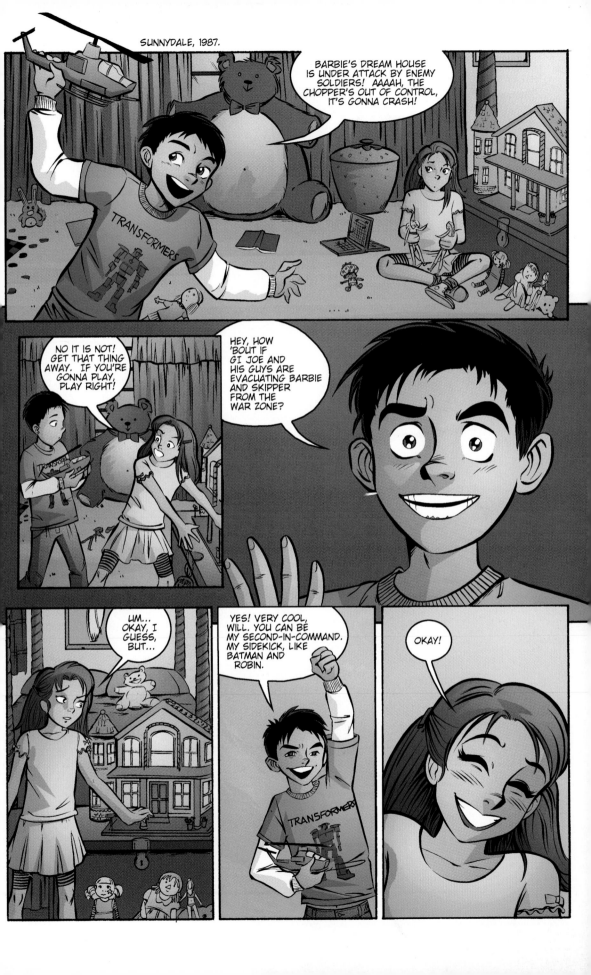

ONCE UPON A TIME, HERE IN SUNNYDALE, CALIFORNIA, THE BATTLE LINES IN THE WAR BETWEEN GOOD AND EVIL WERE SHARPLY DRAWN.

GOOD VERSUS EVIL. LIGHT VERSUS DARKNESS. ORDER VERSUS CHAOS.

THEN, OVER TIME, THINGS BEGAN TO CHANGE. A KIND OF FLOW WAS CREATED BETWEEN THE TWO, ALLIANCES MADE, LOYALTIES ALTERED. BLACK AND WHITE BECAME GREY.

OR AT LEAST THAT WAS HOW IT SEEMED.

APPEARANCES ASIDE, THOUGH, MOST OF THE CREATURES OF THE NIGHT HAVE ONLY ONE LOYALTY ...

... TO THEMSELVES.

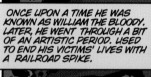

ONCE UPON A TIME HE WAS KNOWN AS WILLIAM THE BLOODY. LATER, HE WENT THROUGH A BIT OF AN ARTISTIC PERIOD. USED TO END HIS VICTIMS' LIVES WITH A RAILROAD SPIKE.

THOUGHT IT WAS COLORFUL, HAVING A SORT OF SIGNATURE LIKE THAT. SPIKE--THAT'S WHAT THEY CALL HIM NOW. HE LIKES THE NAME.

SOMETIMES HE FORGETS HE EVER HAD ANOTHER.

RECENTLY, SOMEONE TINKERED WITH HIS BRAIN. HE CAN'T KILL HUMANS ANYMORE. OF LATE, HE'S BEEN HANGING OUT WITH THE SLAYER AND HER CREW.

IT MAKES HIM FEEL LIKE A PET.

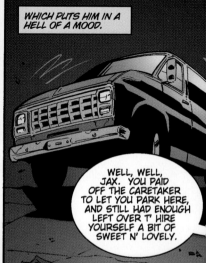

WHICH PUTS HIM IN A HELL OF A MOOD.

WELL, WELL, JAX. YOU PAID OFF THE CARETAKER TO LET YOU PARK HERE, AND STILL HAD ENOUGH LEFT OVER T' HIRE YOURSELF A BIT OF SWEET N' LOVELY.

COME ON, THEN. YOU'VE GOT ALL NIGHT FOR THAT. OL' SPIKE'S IN THE MOOD FOR SOME FUN. LET'S SEE WHAT NIFTY TOYS YOU'VE GOT WITH YOU THIS TIME.

JAX? DON'T KNOW IF YOU REMEMBER, MATE, BUT I'M NOT THE MOST PATIENT--

WHAMMM!

UHNFFF!

YOU HAVE GOT TO BE JOKING.

XERXES THE BLIND. IN SUNNYDALE.

SEE, WILLOW! I TOLD YOU THAT MAD JACK DOESN'T EXIST.

EVEN IF HE DID, I WOULDN'T LET ANYTHING HAPPEN TO YOU. A SUPERHERO ALWAYS HAS TO WATCH OUT FOR HIS FAITHFUL SIDEKICK.

ALL I COULD THINK OF WAS MY MOTHER SAYING IF YOU RAN INTO A BEAR IN THE WILDERNESS YOU SHOULD PLAY DEAD.

I GUESS I CONVINCED MYSELF IT WAS A BEAR. SOME OTHER SIGHTINGS THAT YEAR MADE THE NEWS ...

... BUT EVERYBODY SAID IT WAS A HOAX. THEN HE WENT INTO HIBERNATION, OR WHATEVER, AND THE STORIES STOPPED. OVER TIME, I GUESS I SORT OF BLOCKED IT OUT.

UNTIL ALL THIS.

SO, YOU SAVED MY LIFE WHEN WE WERE EIGHT YEARS OLD, BUT DIDN'T BOTHER TO MENTION IT.

YOU HAD THAT WHOLE SUPERHERO THING HAPPENING. I DIDN'T WANT TO BREAK UP THE DYNAMIC DUO.

SO WE'RE THE SUPERFRIENDS NOW? GREAT. LISTEN, I'M NOT GOING TO BE MISS TERRITORIAL BECAUSE SOMEONE ELSE IS KILLING DEMONS IN MY TOWN.

BUT OUR NEWLY ARRIVED MONSTER MASTER ALSO KILLED BRAD CAULFIELD, WHICH WAS A BIG NO-NO. WE'RE GONNA FIND THIS GUY, CLARIFY THE RULES FOR HIM. VIOLENTLY.

BEFORE WE DO THAT, THOUGH, I WANT TO POKE AROUND MAD JACK'S LAIR.

GILES, YOU AND XANDER COME WITH ME. MAKE SURE THE LITTLE JUMP-THE-GUN DEMON DOESN'T POSSESS ME AGAIN. WILLOW, IF YOU COULD--

I DON'T THINK SO. DID YOU NOT LISTEN TO A WORD I JUST SAID? GILES STARTED THE RESEARCH, HE CAN CONTINUE IT, RIGHT? IT MAKES MORE SENSE FOR ME TO GO WITH YOU.

I STOPPED BEING GILLIGAN TO XANDER'S SKIPPER A LONG TIME AGO. I'M JUST ME, NOW, AND I CAN TAKE CARE OF MYSELF.

OF COURSE YOU CAN, WILLOW. YOU'VE PROVEN YOURSELF DOZENS OF TIMES. IT'S ONLY THAT--

YOU'VE ALREADY STARTED THE RESEARCH, GILES. LOOK INTO MAD JACK, YEAH, BUT CHECK OUT THE DEMON HUNTER'S M.O., TOO. OH, AND GILES ...

BAMM BAMM BAMM!

HMM?

ALL RIGHT, I'M COMING! HANG ON!

BAMM BAMM BAMM!

THE COUNTER! THAT'S THE SECOND TIME I'VE DONE THAT.

THIS HAD BETTER BE GOOD!

TERGAZZI?

THAT'S A NEW LOOK FOR YOU, ISN'T IT? HEY, DO I SMELL SCONES?

"THE SPIRITS KNOW ONLY WHAT THEY HAVE HEARD ALONG THE GHOST ROADS. OF THE DEMON IN THE QUARRY, THEY HAVE TOLD ME ONLY THIS ...

"IT IS CALLED KY-LAAG, AND IT HAS BEEN TRAPPED THERE, FAR BENEATH THE ROCK, FOR CENTURIES, WEAKENED YET FILLED WITH HATE.

"TO CONSERVE ITS STRENGTH, IT SLEEPS FOR TEN YEARS AT A STRETCH, WAKING EACH DECADE TO CALL OUT TO ANY WHO WILL LISTEN, WHO ARE ATTUNED.

"WHISPERING INTO DARK SOULS AND WEAK MINDS, SEARCHING FOR SOMEONE TO SET IT FREE.

"IT IS AN ANCIENT THING, A TRUE DEMON, AND IT YEARNS FOR THE CHAOS AND THE FIRE AND THE FURY OF OLD. IF IT WALKS FREE, DEVASTATION WILL FOLLOW."

THE SPIRITS CANNOT SAY HOW IT CAME TO BE THERE, BUT THEY DO KNOW THIS-- THERE WAS A GUARDIAN, A MONSTER WHO STOOD SENTINEL OVER KY-LAAG.

LUCY HANOVER. ONCE THE SLAYER, SHE HAS BEEN DEAD FOR A CENTURY AND A HALF. SHE WANDERS THE AFTERLIFE, GUIDING LOST SOULS TO THEIR REWARD.

THE GUARDIAN IS DEAD NOW.

BUFFY KILLED HIM.

I'VE BEEN KIDDING MYSELF, WILLOW. ABOUT HAVING A COLLEGE EXPERIENCE. I'VE BEEN PRETENDING.

NO, BUFFY. YOU CAN'T.

IF YOU LEAVE, THAT'S ... IT'S LIKE SAYING YOU DON'T HAVE ANY FUTURE OTHER THAN SLAYING, THAT THERE'S NO BUFFY ANYMORE, JUST THE SLAYER.

MAYBE THAT'S THE WAY IT SHOULD BE. I CAN'T DO IT ALL, WILL.

WHAT, CUZ ONCE YOU DIDN'T DO YOUR SLAYER HOMEWORK? OKAY, KILLING MAD JACK TURNS OUT TO BE A MISTAKE. BUFFY, YOU WERE JUST--

COCKY. TOO SURE I COULD DO IT ALL WITHOUT BREAKING A SWEAT. I HAD IT DOWN. SLAYING. COLLEGE. NO BIG DEAL.

YOU'RE RIGHT, WILL. I DIDN'T DO THE HOMEWORK. IT GOT ME A "D" ON MY HISTORY EXAM. BUT IN SCHOOL, THE ONLY ONE THAT HURTS IS ME.

THE COST OF NOT DOING MY HOMEWORK ON MAD JACK MAY BE THOUSANDS OF LIVES. I WANT A LIFE. BUT I DON'T WANT ANYONE ELSE TO PAY FOR IT.

I'M HEADED UP TO THE QUARRY. I KILLED THE GUARDIAN. UNTIL WE FIGURE OUT HOW TO KEEP KY-LAAG DOWN, I'LL MAKE SURE HE STAYS PUT. LATER.

YEAH.

LATER.

IT'S ALL RIGHT, XIU. I HAVE AN IDEA HOW WE MIGHT FIND HER. STAY WHERE YOU ARE FOR NOW. MAKE CERTAIN HE IS NOT DISTURBED.

ONLY A FEW DAYS, AND HE WILL BE DORMANT AGAIN. THEN WE CAN RETURN HOME. HMM? OH, NO, XIU. NOT WITHOUT KILLING THE SLAYER.

NOT AFTER ALL THE TROUBLE SHE'S CAUSED US. AND SHE KILLED SCIPIO. HE WAS MAD, CERTAINLY, BUT A FAITHFUL PET.

YES ... I'LL BE IN TOUCH.

GOTTA TELL YA, BOSS, I LIKE THE NEW LAIR. VERY CLASSY. SO WHAT'S UP WITH THE GIRLS? ANY NEWS?

SADLY, HIRAM, IT SEEMS THE TWINS HAVE TURNED UP NOTHING ON THE SLAYER. BUT I HAVE A PLAN.

XERXES. MY DEAR ONE, CAN YOU HEAR YOUR MASTER? CAN YOU FEEL ME?

YOU TOUCHED THE VAMPIRE, SPIKE. REACH OUT WITH YOUR MIND AND FIND HIM FOR ME AGAIN. YESSS, THAT'S IT ... TIME FOR AN OLD DEBT TO BE PAID.

"IT'S AN OLD GRUDGE, VENICE, A CENTURY AGO."

MY DARK HEART SWELLS TO SEE YOU ALL GATHERED HERE, MY FRIENDS. THE BLOOD OF CARTHAGE.

FOR YEARS WE HAVE FOUGHT FOR CONTROL OF THIS CITY. THE ASTRIDES ARE POWERFUL ENEMIES, AND MUCH BLOOD HAS BEEN LOST.

NO MORE. THE BATTLE IS OVER. WITH THE SPELLS OF HAMMURABI IN OUR HANDS--

NO.

"THE UGLY BLOKES GOT ME GIRL, SEE. AND I MEAN TO HAVE HER BACK."

MY, MY, WHAT A LOVELY THING YOU ARE.

THE STARS ARE HIDING, AND I THINK THERE'LL BE RAIN. YOU SHOULDN'T HAVE COME IN HERE. SOMEONE'S GOING TO SCREAM.

THAT'S ALL RIGHT, PRETTY. YOU CAN SCREAM ALL YOU LIKE.

YAARRR! GET HER OFF ME! GET HER--

HURRKK!

KRAKKK

IT'S JUST LIKE A LULLABY. AND IT ISN'T OVER YET.

COULD BE. POINT IS THIS--LAST TIME I SAW 'IM, VRAKA HAD A BLOODY ARMY AT HIS DISPOSAL. FROM WHAT I SAW, HE'S DOWN TO THE A-TEAM.

IF THIS KY-LAAG'S AS BAD AS I'VE BEEN TOLD, HE'LL SNAP VRAKA'S BOYS LIKE KINDLING, AND THE SLAYER WON'T FARE MUCH BETTER.

YOU'RE REALLY A GLASS-HALF-EMPTY KINDA GUY, AREN'T YOU, SPIKE? YOU GONNA TRY SWAN DIVING ONTO A BROKEN CHAIR LEG AGAIN, MR. MOPEY?

LISTEN UP, YOU LITTLE TWIT. WHAT I'M SAYING IS AN ALLIANCE COULD BE THE ONLY CHANCE FOR ALL OF US.

YEAH, ESPECIALLY FOR -- UHNFFF!

THUDDD!

KRASSHH!

XANDER!

THIS SEEMS TO BE THE NIGHT FOR UNINVITED GUESTS.

YOU. SOMETHING TELLS ME YOU'RE SPIKE.

AWWW, WHAT GAVE ME AWAY.

KER-ASHH!

VRAKA WANTS THE SLAYER. IT'D BE SIMPLE TO TORTURE THE TRUTH FROM THESE MORTALS...

BUT MY LORD AND MASTER HAS A VENDETTA AGAINST YOU, SPIKE. SO YER GONNA TELL ME WHERE TO FIND THE SLAYER. AND THEN I'M GONNA KILL YOU.

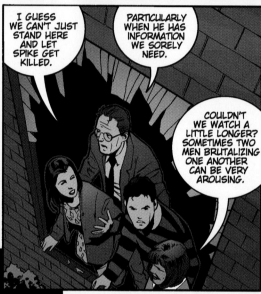

I GUESS WE CAN'T JUST STAND HERE AND LET SPIKE GET KILLED.

PARTICULARLY WHEN HE HAS INFORMATION WE SORELY NEED.

COULDN'T WE WATCH A LITTLE LONGER? SOMETIMES TWO MEN BRUTALIZING ONE ANOTHER CAN BE VERY AROUSING.

NO IDEA WHERE THE LITTLE TROLLOP IS, HONESTLY.

BUT BRING IT ON, STUMPY. YOU'RE TAKIN' ON THE BIG BAD HERE. IT AIN'T BLOODY PLAYTIME.

HARRRR!

"THIS WAS THE END OF THE 19TH CENTURY. ME AN' DRU WERE KNOCKING ABOUT IN VENICE, RAN AFOUL OF A SECT OF ASTRIDES DEMONS. THEY SNATCHED HER."

"BLOOD OF CARTHAGE WERE FEUDING WITH THE ASTRIDES OVER THE CITY. I TOLD VRAKA IF HE HELPED ME, I'D GET HIM BACK THE SPELLS OF HAMMURABI, A BOOK THAT'D GONE MISSING."

WHAT WAS THAT? DID YOU HEAR SOMETHING?

"WHAT A BLOODY MESS THAT WAS."

DAMN THAT VAMPIRE. HE STOLE THE BOOK TO FORCE ME TO HELP HIM, NOW HE ABANDONS US TO THE BATTLE LIKE A COWARD ...

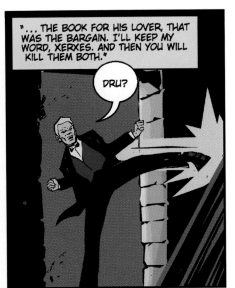

" ... THE BOOK FOR HIS LOVER, THAT WAS THE BARGAIN. I'LL KEEP MY WORD, XERXES. AND THEN YOU WILL KILL THEM BOTH."

DRU?

HELLO, LOVE. YOU CAME FOR ME.

I COULDN'T GET ON WITH- OUT YOU, PET. YOU KNOW THAT.

THERE ARE TOO MANY OF THEM. WE BOUGHT SPIKE ENOUGH TIME. FALL BACK, ALL OF YOU. THIS WAR WILL NOT END TODAY.

YOU GO NO FURTHER.

LIKE HELL.

STOP THEM! YOU CANNOT RUN, SPIKE. I'VE GIVEN YOU WHAT YOU WANT, NOW YOU WILL RETURN WHAT YOU STOLE! I WANT THAT BOOK.

YOU DIDN'T GIVE ME A THING YOU SILLY GIT. DRUSILLA FREED HERSELF. THE DEAL'S OFF.

I'LL HAVE YOUR HEAD, SPIKE! I'LL--- ARRGHHH!

COURSE I NEVER HAD THE BOOK TO BEGIN WITH, BUT I KNEW WHO STOLE IT. WE GOT OUT OF VENICE RIGHT QUICK AFTER THAT ONE.

AND YOU HONESTLY THINK VRAKA WOULD BE WILLING TO MAKE A TRUCE WITH YOU? HE PROBABLY HATES YOU MORE THAN HE DOES BUFFY.

POSSIBLE. I SUPPOSE THAT ALL DEPENDS ON HOW BADLY HE WANTS TO STOP THIS KY-LAAG.

SO WHAT'S THE DEAL WITH KY-LAAG? WHY WOULD VRAKA PLAY PRISON WARDEN ALL THESE YEARS?

GOT ME, GIRLY. YOU'RE ON YOUR OWN WITH THAT ONE.

I KNOW YOU'RE AGAINST IT, BUFFY, BUT PERHAPS SPIKE ISN'T AS MAD AS HE SEEMS. IT DOES SEEM THAT VRAKA'S PRIMARY GOAL IS THE SAME AS OUR OWN.

THAT WOULD BE STOPPING KY-LAAG OF COURSE, RATHER THAN THE GOAL THAT INVOLVES KILLING BUFFY.

OKAY, LOOK, SPIKE'S A LIAR AND A KILLER, AND, OKAY, VAMPIRE, BUT HE DOES HAVE A POINT. WILLOW AND GILES FOUND THAT SPELL TO REBIND KY-LAAG ...

WHICH, LET'S NOT FORGET, REQUIRES SOME ELEMENTS I'LL NEED EVERYONE'S HELP GATHERING. KINDA HARD TO FOCUS ON THAT WHILE BEING HUNTED.

ALL RIGHT. POINT VERY TAKEN. I'M ON BOARD WITH THE TRUCE IDEA. NOW THAT I KNOW JUST TALKING TO THIS DEMON COULD COST SPIKE HIS LIFE, IT'S GOT A LOT MORE APPEAL.

NOW, HERE'S WHAT WE'RE GOING TO DO ...

I HEARD A DEMON TALKING 'BOUT HOW HE'D SWIPED IT, AND USED IT TO MY ADVANTAGE. THAT'S ALL.

THAT'S ALL? THAT'S WORSE!

HHURKKK!

KRANKK!

KRUNCHHHH!

DO YOU HAVE ANY IDEA HOW MANY OF MY FOLLOWERS DIED THAT NIGHT? JUST SO YOU COULD GET YOUR GIRL BACK. AND WHERE IS SHE NOW?

I'D HOLD MY TONGUE RIGHT THERE, OLD MAN. LOOK, I TOLD YOU, I CAME TO TALK. AND I DIDN'T COME ALONE.

KRASHHHHH!

NEW YORK CITY. THE BIG APPLE.

I CAN'T BELIEVE I'M GOING TO NEW YORK. OKAY, IT'S FOR Y'KNOW, HOURS, AND I WON'T BE ABLE TO DO ANYTHING COOL, BUT ... NEW YORK!

YES, WELL, IT'S NICE THAT YOU'RE SO EXCITED, WILLOW. I'M AFRAID I'LL HAVE TO CONTAIN MY ENTHUSIASM UNTIL WE'VE COMPLETED OUR MISSION.

ARE YOU A REAL-LIFE HOOLIGAN, MISTER? LIKE THE TOYS? I'VE GOT SEVENTEEN OF 'EM AT HOME, BUT THEY DON'T MAKE 'EM NO MORE.

TELL ME AGAIN WHY WE HAD TO BRING HIM?

WE HAVE, FOR THE MOMENT, AGREED TO ALLY OURSELVES WITH THE BLOOD OF CARTHAGE. VRAKA WANTED ONE OF HIS PEOPLE ALONG. HE'S A BIT CONSPICUOUS, BUT MIGHT PROVE USEFUL.

COME ON, MISTER? ARE YOU A HOOLIGAN. A REAL ONE? YOU SURE LOOK LIKE ONE.

HRRRMM.

... SO WE'RE GOING THROUGH THE KAMA SUTRA, TRYING ALL THE POSITIONS, BUT WE ONLY GOT TO PAGE SEVENTY-TWO BEFORE HE COLLAPSED.

AT FIRST, I THOUGHT IT WAS ME. THAT DESPITE THE DOZENS OF VARIATIONS AND MY WILLINGNESS TO DUPLICATE ANYTHING WE'VE SEEN ON TAPE ...

... THAT, SOMEHOW, XANDER NO LONGER ENJOYED SEX WITH ME.

NOW, THOUGH, I REALIZE THAT IT'S HIM. APPARENTLY IF WE HAVE THE SEX TOO OFTEN I COULD BREAK HIM. I WAS RELIEVED, BUT ALSO DISAPPOINTED.

Y'KNOW, IT'S NICE OUT HERE, BUT I CAN'T BELIEVE YOU'VE SPENT ALL THIS TIME ON GUARD DUTY WITH NO ONE TO TALK TO. HOW LONELY.

NEW YORK CITY. THE BUILDING IS OWNED BY THE COUNCIL OF WATCHERS. IT IS A WAY STATION OF SORTS FOR MANY OF THEIR OPERATIONS IN NORTH AMERICA.

RUPERT. I TOLD YOU NOT TO COME HERE. I CAN'T HELP.

LOOK, ALLAN, AT LEAST OFFER ME A CUP OF TEA AND A CHANCE TO EXPLAIN. YOU OWE ME THAT MUCH.

IT IS GOOD TO SEE YOU, RUPERT. AND I KNOW THAT I OWE YOU. BUT YOU'RE NOT A MEMBER OF THE COUNCIL ANYMORE.

I CANNOT LET YOU HAVE THE EYE OF PERSIA, EVEN ON LOAN.

I'M TRULY SORRY IT HAS TO COME TO THIS. I THANK YOU FOR THE TEA, ALLAN, HOWEVER ...

... DO IT NOW!

KRACKK!!!

THE COUNCIL WILL HAVE HIM TERMINATED FOR THIS.

EVEN IF HE RETURNS THE AMULET, THERE WILL BE REPERCUSSIONS* FROM THIS ...

"... THOUGH HE WOULDN'T HAVE LET THE LITTLE TROLL KILL ME. NOT RUPERT."

"OLD RIPPER YOU MEAN? ARE YOU CERTAIN? AFTER THIS, I DON'T THINK I KNOW HIM AT ALL. OR IF I EVER DID."

BRRINGALINGA... ...ALINGALING!

WHAT IS THAT? DIDN'T I DO THE SPELL RIGHT?

YOU DID THE SPELL PERFECTLY FINE. SAVED US FROM THE DAGGERS OF KHARTUN, AMONG OTHER THINGS. THAT SOUND IS A TRADITIONAL BURGLAR ALARM.

DAMN ME FOR NOT THINKING OF IT.

THE OTHER HUMANS IN THERE SEEMED TO THINK YOU WOULD SUFFER FOR HAVING DONE THIS.

DID THEY? DOUBTLESS THEY'RE RIGHT. BUT THAT'S A PROBLEM FOR ANOTHER DAY. FOR THE MOMENT, WE MUST HURRY TO CATCH OUR FLIGHT BACK TO ...

SUBWAY

* FOR MORE ON THOSE REPERCUSSIONS, SEE THE GILES ONE-SHOT.

"BUT, OH, THERE WAS A TIME WHEN I WAS WORSHIPPED AND THE BLOOD OF CARTHAGE THREATENED THE WORLD LIKE NO OTHER FORCE OF DARKNESS EVER HAD.

"IT WAS 149 B.C. AND WE WERE BUILDING AN EMPIRE, TO RE-PLACE THE CURRENT HUMAN EMPIRE.

"ROME HAD DEFEATED CARTHAGE'S HUMAN LEADERS, STOLEN AWAY HER POWER ... AND MADE IT SIMPLE FOR ME TO MAKE CARTHAGE MY OWN."

YOU'RE CERTAIN, GENERAL? IT SEEMS ALMOST TOO FANTASTIC, CARTHAGE RULED BY ... MONSTERS.

QUITE CERTAIN, CATO. YOUR SENATE MUST ACT BEFORE THE DEMONS' POWER SPREADS.

AGREED, GENERAL. I WILL SEE TO IT. CARTHAGE MUST BE DESTROYED.

IT WILL BE DONE, SENATOR. I SWEAR IT.

HOW CAN THIS BE? HOW HAVE THE ROMANS DISCOVERED OUR PRESENCE SO QUICKLY?

WE DO NOT KNOW, LORD VRAKA. THE SENATE IS SENDING GENERAL SCIPIO AEMILIANUS WITH ORDERS TO RAZE THE CITY, TO EXPUNGE THE ... YOU, MY LORD.

WE SHALL SEE ABOUT THAT.

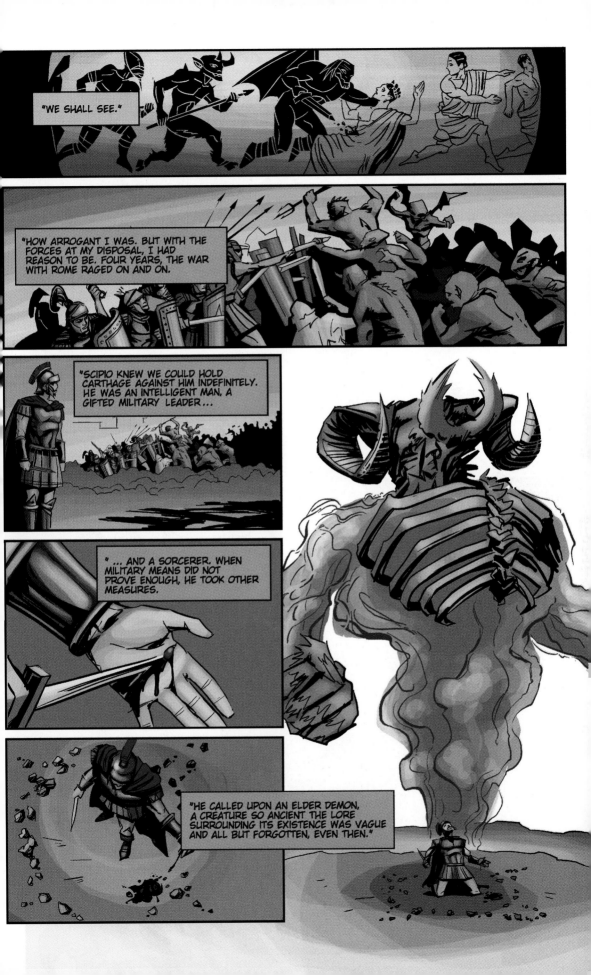

NOW, DO I HAVE ANY VOLUNTEERS TO HELP DECORATE THE CLASSROOM FOR THE SCIENCE FAIR?

ME AN' WILLOW WOULD LOVE TO HELP, MISS FOSTER.

WE WOULD? I MEAN ... YEAH, WE WOULD, BUT ... YOU WOULD?

YOU KNOW WE'RE ONLY HERE BECAUSE YOU HAVE SUCH A CRUSH ON HER. WHY DON'T YOU JUST ADMIT IT?

I'M NOT SEEING THE WRONG-NESS THERE, WILL. THE DECORATING GETS DONE. YOU SCORE POINTS, AND I GET TO BE NEAR MISS FOSTER.

OOOOH. I WILL NEVER UNDERSTAND COMPUTERS. MY SCREEN JUST COMPLETELY FROZE.

NEVER FEAR, MISS FOSTER. WILLOW'S HERE! MY ERSTWHILE AMIGA AND COMPUTERS ARE A MATCH MADE IN TECHNO-HEAVEN. TRUST ME, SHE'S GOT THE MAGIC TOUCH!

THAT'S ... THAT'S WONDERFUL, XANDER, AND HOW SWEET OF YOU TO SAY SO. IS IT TRUE, WILLOW? CAN YOU HELP?

I DON'T KNOW ABOUT THE MAGIC PART, MISS FOSTER, BUT I ... I'LL TRY TO HELP. IF, YOU KNOW, YOU WANT ME TO.

XIU!! NO!

DAMN YOU, KY-LAAG! FOR ALL YOU HAVE TAKEN FROM ME! FOR THE CENTURIES OF PAIN YOU HAVE CAUSED! I SWEAR I WILL NOT REST UNTIL YOU ARE--

UNGHHHHH!

KRUNKKKK

"OKAY, WILL. SLEEP SPELL, CHECK. MEMORY THING, ASSUMING ALSO A CHECK. FIXINGS FOR SENDING THE MASSIVE, HIDEOUS DEMON WHO IS GETTING *BIGGER* BACK HOME?"

WORKING ON IT, XANDER. I'M WORKING ON IT.

I'M NOT TOUCHING THE DEMON DUNG AGAIN. I THINK IT'S YOUR TURN TO TOUCH THE DEMON DUNG.

IT ISN'T MY DEMON DUNG. IT ISN'T EVEN MY TOWN.

WILLOW? I BELIEVE EVERYTHING IS PREPARED. AND ... THIS WOULD BE A GOOD TIME TO MOVE IT ALL. RIGHT NOW.

KEEYYAAAHHH!

KRASSHH!

XANDER!

WILLOW, LOOK--

UNGHH!

NO, NO, NO. NOT NOW.

THE REST OF IT'S GIVING WAY!

THROUGH ME BLOWS THE RAGING WIND, MY SPIRIT IS DRAWN BY THE POWER OF THE MOON. HOLD BACK THE STORM. HOLD BACK THE EARTH. HOLD BACK THE DARK.

XANDER. GET THE DUNG. IF IT GETS BURIED, WE WON'T HAVE TIME TO GET MORE.

AW, COME ON! "HEY, NEED SOMEONE TO PICK UP SOME DUNG? CALL XANDER. HE'S YOUR MAN FOR DUNG!"

SOME WEREN'T SO LUCKY.

GOODBYE, BUFFY. REMEMBER WHAT I SAID. ABOUT LIFE. IF YOU EVER NEED ME, WILLOW CAN REACH ME. EVEN JUST TO TALK. EVEN IF YOU JUST FEEL ... LOST.

THANKS, LUCY. FOR EVERYTHING. I'M SORRY YOU COULDN'T ... STAY. IT'S HARD WORK, THE WHOLE LIVING THING, LIKE ONE LONG BATTLE. BUT WHAT ARE WE WITHOUT IT?

"GHOSTS, BUFFY. JUST GHOSTS."

... SUNNYDALE STILL CLEANING UP AFTER A FREAK TORNADO THAT TOUCHED DOWN BRIEFLY IN THE-- >CLICK<

THIS IS BORDERING ON THE LOONY, YOU GUYS. I DON'T CARE HOW MANY TIMES SHE SAID IT, WE SHOULD NEVER HAVE LET HER GO TO FACE VRAKA ALONE.

BUFFY INSISTED, XANDER. VRAKA VOWED HE WOULD NOT HAVE XERXES WITH HIM.

SHE BELIEVES HIM NOBLE ENOUGH TO KEEP HIS WORD.

BUFFY FELT SHE COULD DO NO LESS. I BELIEVE SHE ALSO WANTED TO ... CLOSE THIS CHAPTER OF HER LIFE THE WAY SHE BEGAN IT. ON HER OWN. MUCH AS IT PAINS US ...

"... WE MUST RESPECT HER WISHES."

I'M HERE.

IT'S TIME.

IT'S FINALLY OVER FOR YOU.

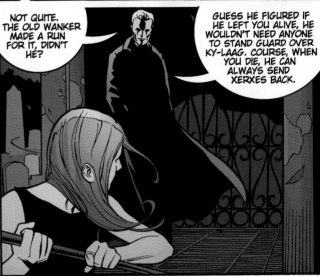

NOT QUITE. THE OLD WANKER MADE A RUN FOR IT, DIDN'T HE?

GUESS HE FIGURED IF HE LEFT YOU ALIVE, HE WOULDN'T NEED ANYONE TO STAND GUARD OVER KY-LAAG. COURSE, WHEN YOU DIE, HE CAN ALWAYS SEND XERXES BACK.

HE'S GONE?

DON'T GET ALL MISTY. WOULDN'T HAVE BEEN MUCH OF A CHALLENGE FOR YOU, NOW WOULD HE? VRAKA'S LONG PAST HIS PRIME, INTO HIS TWILIGHT CENTURIES AND ALL.

NOT THAT WATCHING YOU KILL HIM WOULDN'T HAVE BEEN A HOWL, MIND. BUT I'M GLAD TO BE QUIT OF THE BUZZARD. THERE'S NOTHING TO BE GAINED FROM LIVING IN THE PAST ...

"... GOTTA MOVE FORWARD. THAT'S THE TRICK, SEE."

BUFFY! HEY! IS THIS COMING-FOR-A-VISIT BUFFY, OR MAYBE-I'LL-GIVE-THIS-COLLEGE-THING-ANOTHER-SHOT BUFFY? 'CAUSE THE JACKET GIVES ME HOPE.

I'M THE ... I MEAN IT'S THE SECOND ONE.

THAT IS SO ... A VERY TINY "YAY," BUT ONLY BECAUSE SQUEALING WITH JOY MIGHT BRING PARAMEDICS. YOU HAVE NO IDEA HOW GLAD I AM THAT YOU'RE BACK.

I AM, AREN'T I? BACK TO LIFE. HAVING ONE, I MEAN. YOUNG, WILD, AND AT LEAST PARTIALLY FREE--

"--IT'S OF THE GOOD."

THE END

The Art of
The Blood of Carthage

I like to think this was the most ambitious *Buffy* project we'd tackled at the time. When it was time to take the *Buffy* comic into its twenties, we were wrapping up a very complex story arc called *Bad Blood*, collected in three volumes – *Bad Blood*, *Crash Test Demons*, and *Pale Reflections*. We'd tried modeling a story arc after the TV show, with a year-long plot gradually built around other side adventures. I decided to go after a different structure: the novel.

The first step in creating this book was asking Christopher Golden to plot a story with the same scope as one of his *Buffy* novels, but with the visual opportunities of a film. So while this section is all about the art of the book, every design contained here had its origin in a panel description by Chris.

During the *Bad Blood* run on *Buffy*, when Jef Matsuda was doing all the covers, he and I had talked about having him design characters for the series. We worked out a deal in which his payment for drawing the covers would include some design work on original characters. *Blood of Carthage* would be the first story in which we'd exercise that deal.

Buffy #21 cover design and final art, by Matsuda with Sibal and Major

Spike "audition" by Horton

Art by Richards

Cliff Richards was set to be the artist on the series, and so *Blood of Carthage* would mainly be his responsibility. He'd only drawn about six monthly comics for me at that point, with two fill-in issues breaking up his run, so I was still unsure of his ability to keep a monthly schedule. (It turns out my fears were completely unwarranted. Cliff is the fastest artist I've ever worked with, constantly turning in work well before the deadline. But in August of 1999, I didn't know that.) So I worked out with Chris that the flashback scenes of Willow as a kid and Spike and the Blood of Carthage in the past would be drawn by other artists. Chynna Clugston-Major had done a pinup in that year's *Buffy Annual* which people seemed to like, so she was chosen for the Willow flashbacks. Ryan Sook's first *Spike and Dru* comic had caused quite a stir, so it was decided that he would handle the darker flashbacks, featuring Spike. Ryan's schedule got in the way, and Brian Horton and Paul Lee were brought in. Brian is an artist for Dreamworks Interactive, and Paul is an artist I've known since 1991, when I was working for a literary magazine called Glimmer Train Press.

When Chris's outline was finalized, various characters and scenes were assigned to the different artists. When drawing a comic, the artist has to design literally hundreds of things. Cliff Richards, in drawing this book, designed the quarry, the Quarry House, and a dozen demons and other monsters. Those designs are done on the fly, under the pressure of monthly deadlines, and there's no time for the kind of documentation that we're able to provide for the other artists on the book. So while this section focuses on the contributions of Jeff, Brian, and Paul, they'd all quickly admit that *Blood of Carthage* is without a doubt Cliff's book, beginning to end. They've just served to enrich the feel of it, and vary the vision.

The first drawings to be done for *The Blood of Carthage* were Jeff Matsuda's character and first cover designs. Jeff nailed Mad Jack the first time, and we never altered the design from there. Ky-Laag was a little harder. I wanted a demon unlike anything we'd ever seen in comics before, and Jeff and I went over a lot of ideas. Having parts of his body made of smoke was something we thought we'd never seen before, and it became the crux of the design.

Ky-Laag

Buffy #25 cover by Matsuda with Owens and Major—the first finished drawing of Ky-Laag

Hardest of all was Vraka. A lot of designs were proposed and scrapped for the character before we settled on the final design. Of all the characters Jeff designed for the book, Vraka would appear the most, and would have the most influence on the plot.

Mad Jack

Vraka

Brian Horton was eager to design characters for the book as well, but by the time he was brought on board, Jeff had already done most of the new characters, and I wanted to leave some for Cliff. Since Brian was doing the Blood of Carthage flashbacks, I decided to let him design Xerxes, another character who needed a real unique look. Brian's paintings and sketches were given to Cliff, since it was actually Cliff who had to draw the character first. In order to draw the pages featuring Spike, he had to meet with James Marsters's approval. Those pieces piqued the interest of Joss Whedon, which led to Brian's further work on the *Buffy* license.

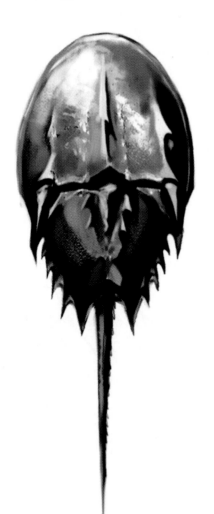

Xerxes the Blind by Horton